Scottish Wildlife

A Colouring Book

Elfreda Crehan

Published 2024 by Lexus Ltd
47 Broad Street, Glasgow G40 2QW

Reprinted 2025

www.lexusforlanguages.co.uk

Cover design by Elfreda Crehan

British Library Cataloguing in Publication Data.
A catalogue record for this book is available from the British Library.

ISBN: 9781904737650

Printed in the UK by Ashford Colour Ltd

MIX
Paper | Supporting responsible forestry
FSC® C011748
FSC www.fsc.org

Scotland's wildlife can be found in all sorts of places – from mountain top to under the sea, from the city to the forest floor. Colour in the pictures and learn some Scots wildlife words, new and old ...

tammy norrie
partan
clockladdie
hurcheon
wyver
ousel
kye
bull-ether
rowan
hoolet
whitrat
puddock
gowk
neesik

on the cliff top

bonxie
Arctic skua

tammy norrie
puffin

gressy spink
sea pink

along the seashore

partan
crab

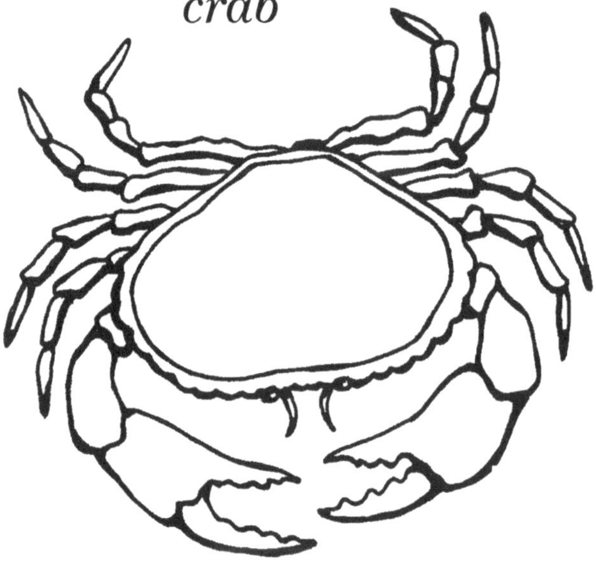

shalder
oyster catcher

selkie
seal

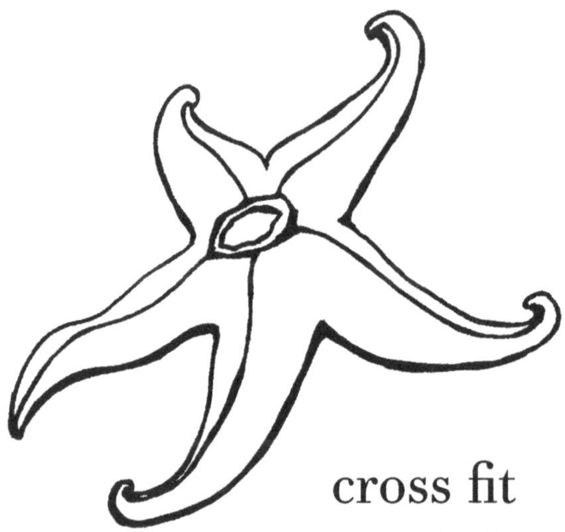

cross fit
starfish

on the forest floor

clockladdie
ladybird

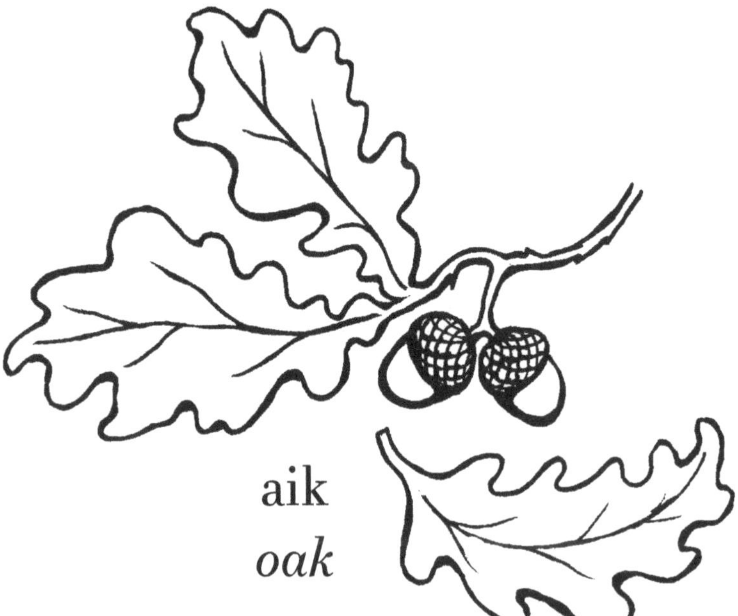

aik
oak

mairten
pine marten

in the hedgerow

bumbee
bumblebee

bramble
blackberry

hurcheon
hedgehog

brock
badger

in the city

tod
fox

wyver
spider

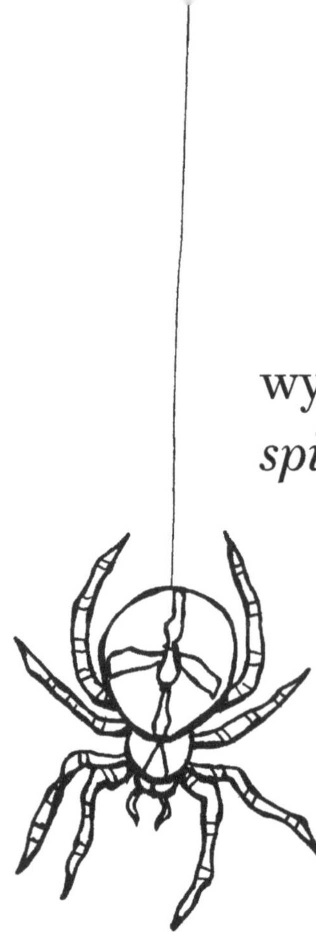

ratton
rat

dentylion
dandylion

in the garden

mavis
thrush

ousel
blackbird

croodlin doo
woodpigeon

wirm
worm

mowdie
mole

at the lochside

on the mountain

bizzart
buzzard

rowan
mountain ash

white hare
mountain hare

on the moor

reid deer
red deer

bull-ether
dragonfly

edder
adder

broom
gorse

in the kirkyard at night

moch
moth

hoolet
owl

flichtermoose
bat

in the field

maup
rabbit

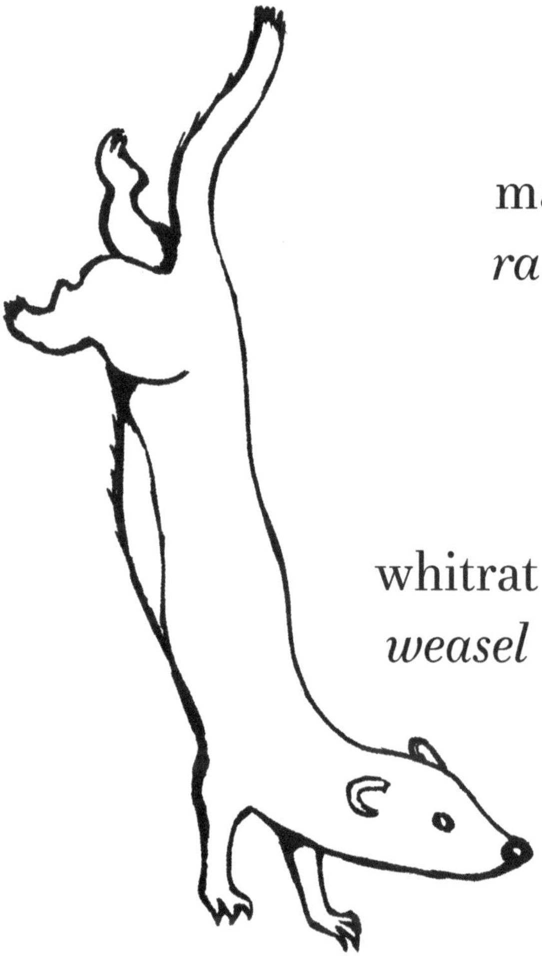

whitrat
weasel

moose
mouse

along the riverbank

butterie
butterfly

puddock
frog

harebells
bluebells

watterdug
water vole

in the tree tops

bunnet fir
Scots pine

gowk
cuckoo

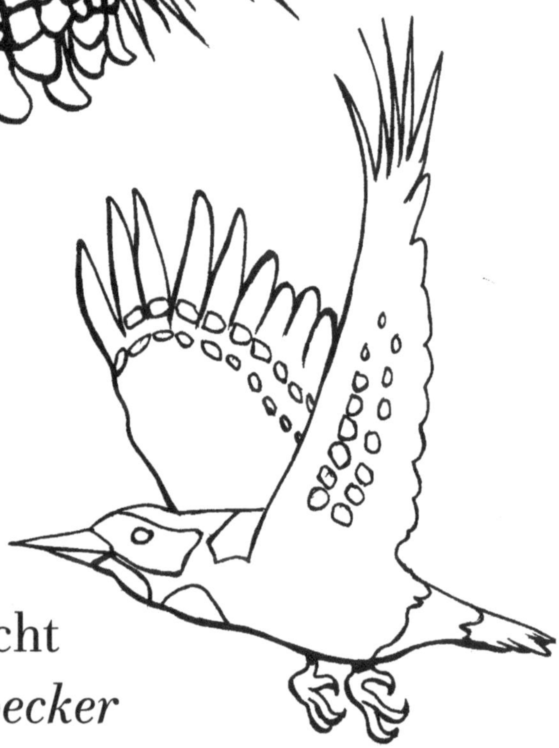

specht
woodpecker

con
squirrel

under the sea

black dooker
cormorant

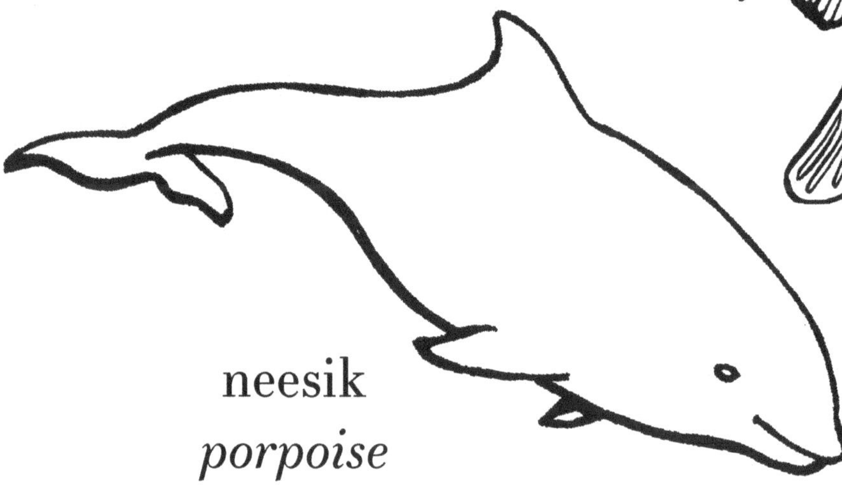

neesik
porpoise

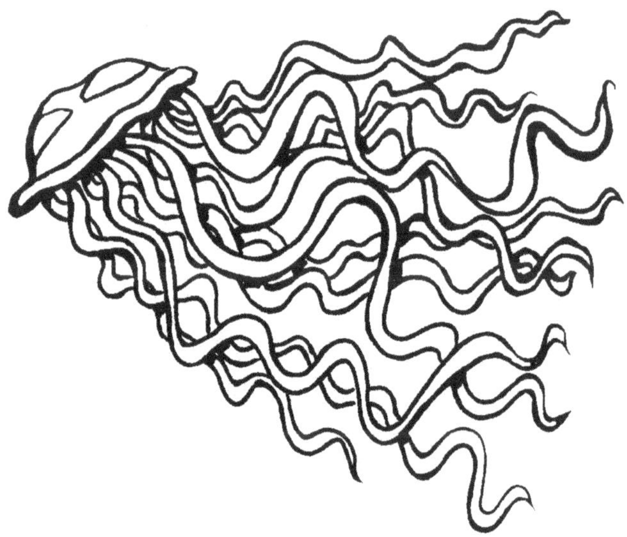

selkie's blubber
jellyfish

muldoan
basking shark

in the skies

erne
eagle